D1107216

MONSTERS

For Craig, Molly, and Jesse, of course

—Lynn

SLEEPING BEAR PRESS™

www.sleepingbearpress.com © Sleeping Bear Press • Printed and bound in the United States • 10 9 8 7 6 5 4 3 2 1
Library of Congress Cataloging-in-Publication Data • Names: Becker, Lynn, 1960- author. | Brundage, Scott, illustrator.
Title: Monsters in the briny / written by Lynn Becker ; illustrated by Scott Brundage.
Description: Ann Arbor, MI : Sleeping Bear Press, [2022] | Audience: Ages 4-8. |
Summary: In this variation on the traditional sea shanty "What Do You Do with," a ship's crew of sailors must contend with mythical sea
creatures, including a kraken, a sea serpent, and a giant tortoise. • Identifiers: LCCN 2021037584 | ISBN 9781534111493 (hardcover)
Subjects: LCSH: Children's songs, English—United States—Texts. | Sea songs—Texts. | CYAC: Sea monsters—Songs and music. | Songs. |
LCGFT: Picture books. | Sea shanties. | Song texts. • Classification: LCC PZ8.3.B39182 Mo 2022 | DDC 782.42—dcE 23/eng/20211107
LC record available at https://lccn.loc.gov/2021037584

IN THE BRINY

By Lynn Becker ★ Illustrated by Scott Brundage

PUBLISHED BY SLEEPING BEAR PRESS™

What do you do with a grumpy kraken?
Crabby, cranky, crusty kraken?
What do you do with a grumpy kraken?
kraken in the briny.

Share some jokes and your best **riddle**,
Feed her cakes from Cookie's **griddle**,
Teach her how to bow the **fiddle**,

kraken in the briny.

Yo! Ho! And ARRR! We're flooding,
Yo! Ho! The deck is mudding,
Yo! Ho! Our anchor's thudding,

Kraken in the briny.

What do you do with a scruffy sea goat?
Messy, mussy, mucky sea goat?
What do you do with a scruffy sea goat?

Sea goat in the briny.

Comb his forelock, curl his **lashes**,
Wind him round with fancy **sashes**,
Hope the silk won't give him **rashes**,

Sea goat in the briny.

Yo! Ho! Our feet are slipping,
Yo! Ho! The sail is ripping,
Yo! Ho! Our ship is tipping,

Sea goat in the briny.

What do you do with a sickly serpent?
Ill, unwell, and bilious serpent?
What do you do with a sickly serpent?

Serpent in the briny.

Keep a bucket at the **ready**,
Mop his forehead if he's **sweaty**,
Tuck him into serpent **beddy**,

Serpent in the briny.

Yo! Ho! The sea is stewing,
Yo! Ho! Our ship is slewing,
Yo! Ho! We're all snafuing,

Serpent in the briny.

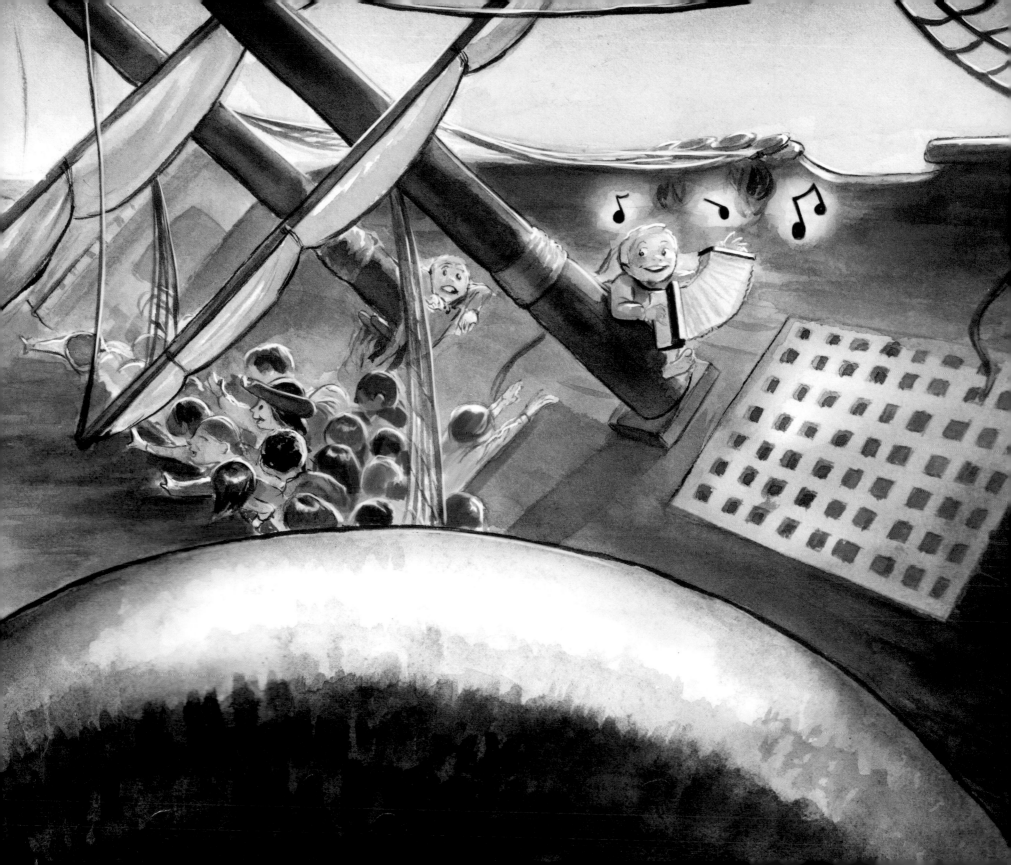

What do you do with a tearful turtle? Gloomy, downcast, dismal turtle? What do you do with a tearful turtle? **Turtle in the briny.**

Spend some splendid time **together**,
Buff her beak with spit and **leather**,
Keep her from the nasty **weather**,

Turtle in the briny.

Yo! Ho! Our ship is **banking,**
Yo! Ho! The wheel is **cranking,**
Yo! Ho! Look out, we're **tanking,**
Turtle in the briny.

What do you do with a hungry Hydra? Starving, famished, hangry Hydra?
What do you do with a hungry Hydra?

Haul him up a net of **fishes,**
Serve them any way he **wishes,**
Plankton gravy is **delicious,**
Hydra in the briny.

Yo! Ho! And up he's rising, Yo! Ho! He's quite surprising,

Yo! Ho! our boat's capsizing, Hydra ... in ... the ...

No more shipwrecking monsters!!!

What do you do with a
grumpy sailor?

Fed-up, put-out,
peevish sailor?

What do you do with a grumpy sailor?

Sailor in the briny.

Clown around and she'll start grinning,
Play the games that she keeps winning,
Stick with her through thick and thinning,
Sailor in the briny.

Yo! Ho! And up we're rising,
Yo! Ho! We're ALL surprising,
Yo! Ho! We're harmonizing,

Monsters in the briny.

★ A Few Words about Sea Shanties ★

Ahoy and avast,* mateys! Listen up. Long before boats had engines, sailors sang sea shanties as they worked aboard their ships. With strong, regular rhythms, these songs helped a crew to heave! and to ho! in unison. Whether hoisting an anchor, raising a sail, or getting all hands to row at once, working together was necessary. Also, the more fun the song, the less boring the job might have seemed!

*By the way, *ahoy* is the way sailors say "hello," and *avast* means "STOP" in sailor lingo!

Now, Here Be Our Monsters

The **Kraken** is a legendary beast that's often described as resembling a giant squid. It terrorizes sailors the world over, but the most experienced lads and lassies know the way to win its heart is with tasty flapjacks, a good joke, and maybe even a song or two. Also, with its many long tentacles, a kraken is very fond of hugs!

The mysterious sea goat called **Capricorn** has the head and upper body of a goat, and the bottom half of a fish. Though making its home in the briny deep, Capricorn is celebrated in the sky as a constellation, and it's even more famous for being a sign of the zodiac. This attention has made it extremely vain, so it prefers to look its best at all times.

Sea serpents are dragons that live in the ocean. They are huge, with long, scaly bodies. Sometimes they have small heads and webbed paws. They love to chase ships, but have delicate stomachs and get seasick easily. Sea serpents may also be referred to as worms, wyrms, or sea dragons.

Aspidochelone (As-pi-dock-a-lone) is a sea turtle so large, it looks more like an island than a beastie. Its shell is covered in rocks, small trees, and even a sandy beach or two. It lures sailors to its shores, then, rising, tips them into the sea. Even though it makes its home in the briny, this sea turtle loves to ride out rainstorms under any number of colorful umbrellas.

The **Hydra** is a scary kind of dragon, with lots of heads, terrible breath, and poisonous blood. If you see a Hydra, you probably want to row the other way. But you can try getting on its good side by serving it—quickly—a meal that includes plankton gravy. Like Capricorn the sea goat, Hydra has a constellation, too!

Monsters in the Briny

(Sung to the tune of "What Shall We Do With a . . .")

What do you do with a grumpy kraken?
Crabby, cranky, crusty kraken?
What do you do with a grumpy kraken?
Kraken in the briny.

Share some jokes and your best riddle,
Feed her cakes from Cookie's griddle,
Teach her how to bow the fiddle,
Kraken in the briny.

Yo! Ho! And ARRR! We're flooding,
Yo! Ho! The deck is mudding,
Yo! Ho! Our anchor's thudding,
Kraken in the briny.